W9-DFT-450

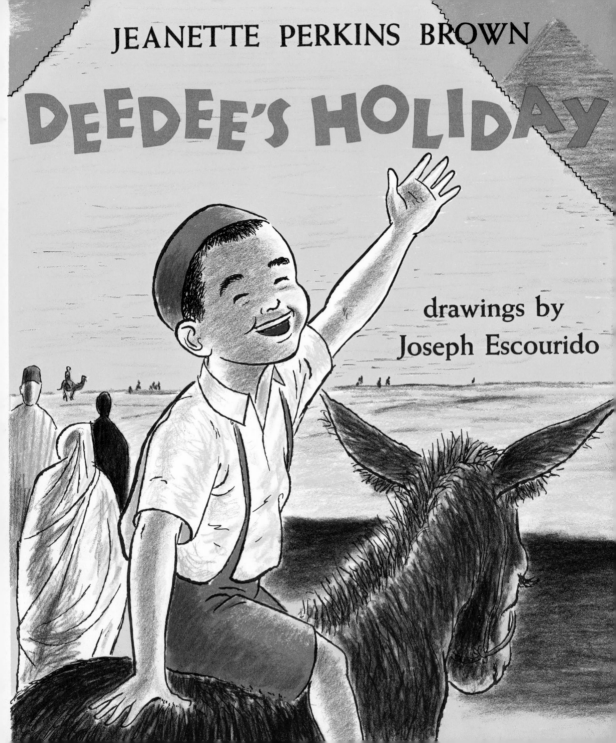

JEANETTE PERKINS BROWN

DEEDEE'S HOLIDAY

drawings by
Joseph Escourido

DEEDEE'S HOLIDAY

by Jeanette Perkins Brown

DRAWINGS BY JOSEPH ESCOURIDO

FRIENDSHIP PRESS   NEW YORK

FORMAT BY DOROTHY PAPY

LIBRARY OF CONGRESS CATALOG CARD NUMBER 56-9248

Deedee woke very early. He sat up in bed and listened. There was singing in the streets. Crack bombs were snapping. Boys were shouting. And in the doorway his brothers, Magedy and Albair, were calling, "Wake up, Deedee! Remember what day it is! See our new clothes!"

He remembered now. It was the Day of Smelling the Pure Air, the happiest holiday in Egypt.

He jumped out of bed. He could hear his mother in the kitchen. She was packing food in a basket.

"I know!" he cried. "We go to the pyramids today for a picnic! We eat with our cousins and ride on donkeys and have ice cream!" Then he saw his new clothes.

"Oo-oo!" he exclaimed. "New shoes, too!" And he hurried to dress himself to be ready.

Papa was waiting to drive the family to the river Nile.

All the people of the city of Cairo seemed to be there, breathing in the sweet air of spring.

Everyone was gay and happy. The bigger boys threw noisy little crack bombs. "Crack! Crack! Pop! Pop!" A girl jumped and screamed and then laughed.

But Deedee was hungry. "I want my breakfast," he said. "Can't we go to the pyramids now?"

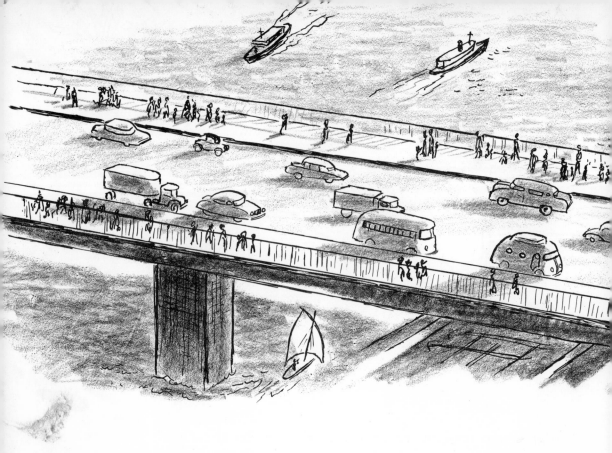

So they climbed into the car again to cross the river on
their way to the pyramids.

The roads were full of people walking and riding. Every-
body was going somewhere in the country to celebrate the
holiday.

Boats of all sizes were on the river. The little ones looked
like butterflies lighting on the water.

"We will park the car near the first pyramid," said Papa,
"and walk until we find our picnic place. The uncles and
aunts and cousins will meet us there. After breakfast you
children may go for a donkey ride around the pyramid."

The crowds were so great that Papa lifted Deedee to his shoulders and carried him.

A tall guard in a white suit with a band on his sleeve smiled at Deedee and lifted his hand in a salute.

Deedee saluted back. "I am tall now. I can see everything," he said proudly. "Oh! Oh! I can see our uncles and cousins waiting for us!"

Sure enough, the uncles and their families were sitting
nearby on rugs spread on the sand. They were already eat-
ing their breakfast. Deedee and his family joined them to
eat the colored eggs, the fish, the lettuce, and the sweet
cakes Mama had brought.

After they had eaten, the cousins played together at
leapfrog and tag and wrestling. They watched the people
passing them on their way to the pyramid.

"Now, may we go for our donkey ride?" the boys asked
their papas.

"And have ice cream afterwards?" Deedee begged.

Papa gave money to Musa, the oldest cousin. "Here is enough for rides and ice cream for all of you," he said, "but you older ones must take good care of the younger ones." To all of them he said, "Hold hands, and keep close together."

The children promised and started off hand in hand in a line, with Musa at the head and Deedee at the end.

They saw many people walking up the sandy path to the first pyramid. Some wore clothes that looked strange to Deedee and his brothers. They spoke in strange languages, using words Deedee could not understand.

Ahead of Deedee was a red-haired American boy with his father and mother.

Deedee and his brothers saw him point to the top of the pyramid and say something excitedly to his father.

They did not understand his words because they spoke Egyptian, but they understood that he was asking about the pyramid. They wanted to tell him that it had been built long ago to help people to remember a famous king.

They looked up at it now. It was very big. It must have
taken a long time to build. Deedee was glad it had been
built, for it was fun to ride around on a donkey. Some day
when he was big like Musa, he would go around on a camel!

Magedy helped him get on a donkey. "I will be right
behind you," he told Deedee.

When they came to the other side of the pyramid, they
saw the Sphinx. The red-haired American boy called out
again, but Deedee could not understand what he said.

"He is talking about the Sphinx," thought Deedee, "but
he uses funny words."

The Sphinx was large, too, but it was different from the pyramids.

"It looks like a big lady with wings behind her ears," thought Deedee, jogging along on his donkey.

He was sorry when the ride was over.

Musa helped Deedee off the donkey and paid money
for their ride.

"Now for ice cream!" called Magedy and Albair.

"Remember," Musa reminded them, "hold hands and
KEEP TOGETHER!"

People crowded around the ice cream stand. Children were squeezing between older people, and families were getting all mixed up.

Musa, at the head of the line, reached the stand first. "I'll get the ice cream," he said. "Stay together."

He passed the first ice cream stick to Deedee, who wriggled himself free of the people around.

Deedee took the stick in both hands and licked the chocolate covering down to the cool ice cream. He did not know that he was moving with the crowd and following some children he had never seen before.

Music sounded in the distance. The children hurried. Deedee hurried, too, until he saw a monkey doing tricks. He looked around to show Magedy. Magedy was not there! Albair was not there! Musa was nowhere in sight!

"Mama!" Deedee cried. "I want my mama!"

The mother of the red-haired boy heard him. She did not understand Deedee's words, but she understood that a little boy had lost his mama.

"We will help you find your mama," she said, taking his hand. Deedee could not understand her words, but he could understand the comfort of her hand and the kindness of her voice.

She led him to a guard in a white suit with a band on his sleeve.

"Hello," said the guard. He saluted Deedee just as he had before.

Deedee blinked through his tears. The guard's salute made him remember the time when he was safe on his papa's shoulders. "I want my papa," he wailed.

"Come, we will find your papa," said the guard.

Of course Deedee could not know that all this time Musa and the others were trying to find HIM. Back at the ice cream stand Musa had paid for the last ice cream stick. "Keep together now," he was saying. Then he noticed something wrong.

"Where is Deedee?" he asked in a worried voice.

"Deedee!" called Magedy. "Deedee!" shouted Albair. In a minute, Deedee's brothers and cousins were searching through the crowds and shouting, "Deedee!"

They looked this way and that way. Where was Deedee? Where had he gone? What had happened? Nobody knew.

"Have you seen a little boy about so high?" they asked
people whom they met.

All around were many little boys about Deedee's size,
but none of them was Deedee.

"Take hold of hands again," called Musa unhappily. "We
must go and tell the family."

The cousins all walked along in a line, every little while
calling in frightened voices, "Deedee! Deedee!" But nobody
answered. The smallest children began to cry. "We have
lost Deedee," they sobbed, when they saw their families.

"Lost Deedee!" Deedee's papa and mama exclaimed, jumping up.

"Lost Deedee!" cried his uncles and aunts. "We must find him at once!"

"I will go this way," said one uncle, pointing.

"I will go that way," said another, pointing in the other direction.

"I will search near the ice cream stand," said Papa.

Just then the red-haired American boy came in sight. He stopped when he saw the children still holding hands. He shouted to someone behind him. Then he disappeared in the crowd.

Magedy looked after him. "That was the American boy
we saw at the pyramid," he said. "He looked excited when
he saw us. Do you suppose he has found Deedee?"

At that very moment the boy came running back, pointing to Deedee's family and shouting to someone back of him.
Deedee's family waited to see what would happen.

Then, high above the heads of other people, appeared a little boy with a paper cap on his head. He was riding on the shoulders of a guard in a white suit with a band on his sleeve.

"Deedee!" went up a glad shout from Deedee's family. Mama and Papa rushed toward him with their arms out.

"How did you find him?" they asked the guard. And he answered, "The Americans here saw your children holding hands in a line. So we looked for such a line."

"Thank God he is found!" said Deedee's mama in Egyptian words.

"Thank God he is safe!" said the red-haired boy's mother in American words.

And each understood what the other mother meant.

"Mama! Papa!" Deedee was saying. "You got lost, and I couldn't find you!"

Mama and Papa laughed. They thought it was Deedee who had gotten lost. But whoever had been lost was found now and was getting a great big hug.

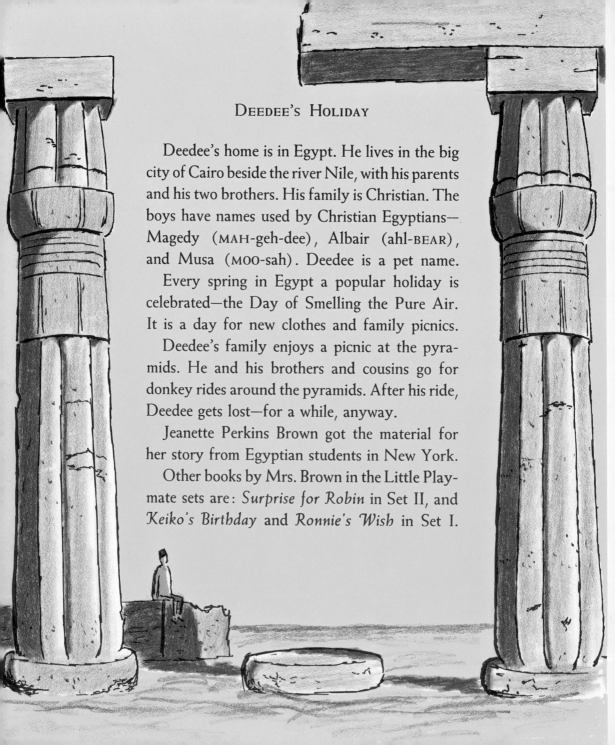

DEEDEE'S HOLIDAY

Deedee's home is in Egypt. He lives in the big city of Cairo beside the river Nile, with his parents and his two brothers. His family is Christian. The boys have names used by Christian Egyptians—Magedy (MAH-geh-dee), Albair (ahl-BEAR), and Musa (MOO-sah). Deedee is a pet name.

Every spring in Egypt a popular holiday is celebrated—the Day of Smelling the Pure Air. It is a day for new clothes and family picnics.

Deedee's family enjoys a picnic at the pyramids. He and his brothers and cousins go for donkey rides around the pyramids. After his ride, Deedee gets lost—for a while, anyway.

Jeanette Perkins Brown got the material for her story from Egyptian students in New York.

Other books by Mrs. Brown in the Little Playmate sets are: *Surprise for Robin* in Set II, and *Keiko's Birthday* and *Ronnie's Wish* in Set I.